Tessa and the Tease

Written by
Amy Syd Babcock

Pictures by
Julie Murphy

For my wonderful husband Phil
with love from your sunshine girl

I'd like to thank my daughter Julie,
whose personal experience with teasing inspired this story;
and my son Saib, who taught me the value of finding the rainbow in people.
I love you both so much! – A.B.

Special thanks go to Julie Murphy for her incredible illustrations
and to my friends and editors for their feedback and contributions:
Ellyn W., Cathy A., Jacki C., Amy B., Rebecca M., Phil B.
and especially Danielle Sunshine. – A.B.

Tessa and the Tease
Text copyright © 2022 by Amy Syd Babcock
Illustrations copyright © 2022 by Julie Murphy
ISBN 978-1-7379336-0-1 (Hardcover)
ISBN 978-1-7379336-1-8 (Paperback)

Book Design by: Lorie DeWorken, MindtheMargins.com

Published by: Amy Syd Babcock

www.amysyd.com

Hi, I'm Tessa.
I'm in the third grade and I love school.
I love school because I love to learn,
especially about science.

And I love
spending time
with my
friends,
especially
my best friend,
Emily.

During recess,
we play games, jump rope,
climb the monkey bars.

It's triple fantastic!

It's my favorite time of day.

But lately,
it's my least favorite,

ever since
Luke started
teasing me.

He teased me
on the bus:
"Hey, Shrimpo!"

He teased me
at my cubby:
"Hey, Peanut.
Are you
growing taller?
No, it's the hat."

AND,
he teased me
at recess:

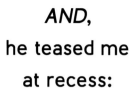

"Oh, excuse me,
Pipsqueak!"

I looked that one up
in the dictionary;
it means small
and insignificant.

I don't love school anymore.

I wanted to make
Luke stop teasing me,
but I didn't know how.

I talked to Emily about it.

"I think you should
ignore him," she said.

I tried that,
but it didn't help.

He still teased me.

The books on the shelf, from left to right:
Young Scientists
Our Solar System
A Little Princess
Ada Twist, Scientist
Smithsonian Science
National Geographic
The Ultimate BUGopedia
The Childrens' Bible
Charlotte's Web

Micro 3000

I talked to my mom about it.

Mom said I should treat Luke
like my little brother Kevie
when he's being a pest.

I say *"STOP!"*
in a very loud voice.

That usually works.

Usually.

Mom also said
I should talk to
my teacher
Ms. Fisher
about it.

But, I'm not
a tattletale.
Not me!

I told her I'll
figure it out.

I love science.
Kids who love science
are good at figuring things out.

So, the next morning,
when Ms. Fisher asked if anyone
would stay in during recess
and help with the autumn
harvest board, I raised my hand.

"I will! I will!"

What a relief to miss recess.

But later,
when our class
visited the library,
Luke held the door
for everyone.

Well,
everyone
but me.

"Oh, I'm sorry, Shrimpo.
I didn't see you,"
and he laughed.

The whole class turned to look at us.

Now, I wished I was invisible.

I was so glad when everyone's attention turned to Ms. Madden. She read to us a story about a pot of gold at the end of a rainbow. When she finished, she asked us to choose a book to take home and then draw pictures of rainbows.

After pulling the first book I saw off the science shelf,
I sat at a table to wait for Emily.

"I wish people were more like rainbows," I told her.
"What do you mean?"

"Rainbows are pretty. They make me feel good.
When Luke calls me names, I always feel bad."

Emily thought about that.

"But people are like rainbows, aren't they?
They have different 'colors.'
Sometimes, they tease. Sometimes, they're kind.
Happy. Sad. Silly."

I stared at Emily.

"You're right.
People do have lots of ways to be."

I turned my paper over.
"Let's see if Luke has a rainbow in him!"

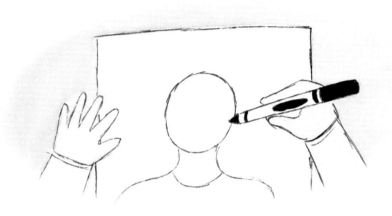

I drew a head and shoulders, then looked over at Luke.

There must be something to like about him.

I liked his hair. It looked reddish-brown and stuck up a little on top.

I liked his bright blue eyes. They were a pretty color.

And I liked his sweatshirt.

It was colorful, like a rainbow.

"He sure likes to make people laugh," I said to Emily.

I wonder if that's why
he teases me.

I was so busy with my
picture that I didn't notice
when it was time to go.

"Hey, Pipsqueak,
wake up!"

I tucked my picture in my book and got in line behind Luke.

"I like your sweatshirt," I said to Luke's back.

I was feeling a little shy.

"What? Oh. I got this on our vacation to California."

"I went to San Francisco once," I said. "It was great."

"You did?"

As the class filed out, Luke began to tell me all about his trip.

When I got home,
I dropped my
backpack by the door
and ran to find Mom.

"Hey Mom, guess what?
School was
triple fantastic!
We drew pictures of
rainbows in the library.
Then I found a rainbow
in Luke . . .

The "Color" List:

Can you find the rainbow in people?
Start with yourself!

___ Kind		___ Good sense of humor
___ Sensitive		___ Good sense of style
___ Creative		___ Good reader
___ Energetic		___ Plays fair
___ Considerate		___ Nice hair
___ Friendly		___ Nice eyes
___ Cheerful		___ Athletic
___ Fun		___ Helpful
___ Funny		___ Patient
___ Smart		___ Good with words
___ Clever		___ Good with numbers
___ Imaginative		___ Good storyteller
___ Artistic		___ _____
___ Enthusiastic		___ _____
___ Honest		___ _____
___ Good listener		___ _____
___ Talented		___ _____
___ Shy		___ _____
___ Good leader		___ _____

Dear Reader,

I hope you enjoyed reading Tessa and the Tease. You probably noticed how Tessa, the main character, changes her relationship with Luke, the boy who teases her. She does this by changing the way she sees him and interacts with him.

She does two things:

1. She studies Luke to see his "colors" or positive traits. She notices how he looks; his expression; his personality; the clothing he wears. (See the list of traits on the previous page for ideas of what to look for in people.)

2. She compliments Luke.

You can do this too if you are having trouble with someone. Ask yourself, "What can I find to like about this person?" It may be tough to find something at first, but then it gets easier. I promise, studying someone's positive traits for even 5 minutes will change the way you see them and how you feel about them. Then it becomes easy to compliment them, and that helps everyone feel better.*

Keep looking for those rainbows!

Amy Syd Babcock
Teacher, Singer-songwriter and Author

*These ideas are based on The Law of Attraction, which means what you think about and pay attention to is what you get more of in your life. By choosing positive thoughts, you can create more positive experiences.

To learn more, see *Sara, Book I, The Foreverness of Friends of a Feather* by Esther and Jerry Hicks.

Please check out my website at www.amysyd.com for:

- free color lists to download
- free rainbows and other scenes from the book to color
- free music to listen to
- the story that inspired this book

Made in United States
Orlando, FL
06 May 2023

32751517R00020